A RHYMING DICTIONARY

TIME to RHYME

by Marvin Terban

illustrated by Chris L. Demarest

Wordsong
Boyds Mills Press

Text copyright © 1994 by Marvin Terban
Illustrations copyright © 1994 by Chris L. Demarest

Published by Wordsong
Boyds Mills Press, Inc.
A Highlights Company
815 Church Street
Honesdale, Pennsylvania 18431
Printed in the United States of America

Publisher Cataloging-in-Publication Data
Terban, Marvin.
   Time to rhyme : a rhyming dictionary / by Marvin Terban ;
illustrated by Chris L. Demarest.—1st ed.
[96]p. : ill. ; cm.
Includes index.
Summary : This title includes a list of words that rhyme, which will help
children to write poems, and examples of poems.
Hardcover ISBN 1-56397-128-3 Paperback ISBN 1-56397-630-7
1. Poetry—Dictionaries. 2. Children's poetry. [1. Poetry.]
I. Demarest, Chris L., ill. II. Title.
808.1—dc20   1994   CIP
Library of Congress Catalog Card Number 93-60242

First Boyds Mills Press paperback edition, 1996
Book designed by Tim Gillner
The text of this book is set in 13-point Galliard.
The illustrations are done in pen and ink.
Reinforced trade edition

10 9 8 7 6 5 4 3 2 1

Reprinted by arrangement with Boyds Mills Press.

To my great-nieces: Shana, Sasha, Amanda, and
Jessica; and my great-nephews: Aaron and Justin.

I do not exaggerate when I say you kids are great!

—M.T.

To Sarah, with love.
    —C.L.D.

Table of Contents

● ●

● ●

About Rhymes and This Book

What Are Rhymes?

Rhymes are words that sound alike at the end. Say "sing," "ring," and "wing." They all have different sounds at the beginning, but they all have the same sound at the end. They rhyme.

Why Use Rhymes?

Rhymes are musical words. They make language sing. Rhymes can add fun and zip to whatever you write. Rhymes can sometimes make things easier to remember, too.

What Rhymes?

Poems sometimes rhyme:

> *One, two,*
> *Buckle my shoe;*
>
> *Three, four,*
> *Shut the door;*
>
> *Five, six,*
> *Pick up sticks;*
>
> *Seven, eight,*
> *Lay them straight;*
>
> *Nine, ten,*
> *A big fat hen.*
> —Mother Goose

Songs often rhyme:

> *Hush, little baby, don't say a word,*
> *Papa's gonna buy you a mockingbird.*
> *If that mockingbird won't sing,*
> *Papa's gonna buy you a diamond ring.*
> *If that diamond ring turns brass,*
> *Papa's gonna buy you a looking glass.*
> —American Folk Song

Greeting cards usually rhyme. They can be serious or funny:

> This card is sent to you, my dear,
> Because I heard you're sick;
> I send you love and lots of cheer,
> And hope you're better quick.

> Happy birthday to you.
> You belong in a zoo.
> You look like a monkey,
> And you act like one, too.

Signs, posters, slogans, and **sayings** are sometimes written in rhyme to help get the messages across with more spark and snap. Rhymes also make them fun to say and easier to remember:

> At two today,
> Come see our play.
> You'll like what you see,
> And the tickets are free!

> The fair starts at eight,
> So don't be late.
> We hate to wait!

> Early to bed and early to rise,
> Makes a man healthy, wealthy, and wise.
> —Benjamin Franklin

How to Use This Book

•••

Think of a word you want to find rhymes for.

Look up that word in the alphabetical list that begins on page 44.

After the word, you will find a page number and a group number. Turn to the page and find that group, and you will see the words that rhyme with your word.

That's all there is to it!

Some Things to Watch Out For

Not all words that rhyme have exactly the same spelling at the end. The following words all rhyme, but notice how differently the same rhyming sound is spelled:

 bird, heard, herd, purred, stirred, word

To make it easy for you to find the rhyming words you need, all the words that rhyme are grouped together no matter how they are spelled.

Let's Try It Out

Suppose you want to make up a song or cheer about your school, and you want it to rhyme. Look up "school" in the alphabetical list. You'll find the words that rhyme with **"school"** on page 33, group 159 ("cool, drool, pool, rule, tool," etc.).

Now think of words that have to do with school and look them up, too:
 read, feed, need, speed, etc. (page 22, group 66)
 write, bright, might, right, etc. (page 30, group 128)
 learn, burn, earn, turn, etc. (page 41, group 227)
 teach, each, reach, speech, etc. (page 20, group 52)

fun, run, sun, won, etc. (page 39, group 214)
play, day, stay, they, etc. (page 19, group 50)
friends, bends, ends, lends, etc. (page 23, group 77)
sports, courts, forts, warts, etc. (page 34, group 175)

By the way, you won't find **"friends"** and **"sports"** on the alphabetical list. But you will find **"friend"** and **"sport."** Just add **"s"** to the words that rhyme with those words.

Play around with all the rhyming words you find. Keep trying different rhyming lines. Remember that the lines you write have to make sense as well as rhyme. Sometimes you won't be able to make up good rhyming lines that make sense. Think of other words. Try finding rhymes for them. Make up new lines. You'll like some of the lines and you'll cross out others. After many tries, you'll have a finished poem, song, cheer, or rap.

We learn all day
And then we play.

On the fields and on the courts,
We are always tops in sports.

We write and write
With all our might.
What we write
Is really bright.

Here we learn
All we need,
How to write
And how to read.

Does Every Line in a Row Have to Rhyme?

When you are writing your poem or song, not every line in a row has to rhyme with the same sound. Here's a famous song in which the ends of lines 1 and 2 rhyme with each other ("thee" and "liberty"). Lines 4, 5, and 6 rhyme with another sound ("died," "pride," and "mountainside"). Lines 3 and 7 rhyme with still another sound ("sing" and "ring").

> *My country 'tis of thee,*
> *Sweet land of liberty,*
> *Of thee I sing.*
> *Land where my fathers died,*
> *Land of the Pilgrims' pride,*
> *From every mountainside,*
> *Let freedom ring.*
>   —Samuel Francis Smith

You could write a song or poem that rhymes like the one above. You can make every other line rhyme with the same sound. Or, the first two lines could rhyme with one sound, and the next two lines could rhyme with another sound. There are lots of possibilities. Whatever sounds good to you is fine.

A Word about Vocabulary

You'll probably know what most of the words in this book mean, but there may be a few you have to look up in the dictionary, like "sphere" or "tweed" or "crave." When you learn what a new word means, you might find that it's just the word you were looking for.

What's Not in This Book

The English language has hundreds of thousands of words. Most of them are not in this book. Only common one-syllable words are in this book. If you can think of longer words that rhyme and make sense, definitely use them.

After you've gotten used to this first rhyming dictionary, you will be able to use a bigger rhyming dictionary that contains longer words and a harder vocabulary. For now, for you, the beginning author, poet, songwriter, or slogan maker, this book should be perfect.

Now it's time to rhyme.

• •

> What does the picture on the cover mean? See page 15, group 12, and you'll know.

Groups of Rhyming Words

1
ah, baa, bah, blah, ha, ma, pa

2
blab, cab, crab, dab, drab, gab, grab, jab, nab, scab, slab, stab, tab

3
ace, base, bass, brace, case, chase, face, grace, lace, pace, place, race, space, trace, vase

4
back, black, crack, jack, knack, lack, pack, quack, rack, sack, shack, smack, snack, stack, tack, track, whack

5
act, backed, cracked, fact, jacked, lacked, packed, pact, quacked, smacked, snacked, stacked, tacked, tact, tracked, whacked

6
ad, add, bad, dad, fad, glad, had, lad, mad, pad, plaid, sad

7
aid, blade, braid, fade, glade, grade, laid, made, maid, paid, prayed, preyed, raid, shade, spade, sprayed, stayed, strayed, swayed, they'd, trade, wade, weighed

Jack has a cracker snack,
While sitting in his shady shack.
He packs his snack up in his sack,
And wears it to the shack and back.

8
calf, graph, half, laugh, staff

9
craft, draft, laughed, raft

10
bag, brag, drag, flag, gag, hag, nag, rag, sag, shag, snag, stag, tag, wag

11
age, cage, gauge, page, rage, sage, stage, wage

12
ail, ale, bail, bale, braille, fail, frail, gale, grail, hail, hale, jail, mail, male, nail, pail, pale, quail, rail, sail, sale, scale, snail, stale, tail, tale, they'll, trail, veil, wail, whale

● ● ● ● ● ● ● ● ● ● ● ● ● ●

Can't afford a plane to Spain?
Why not take a train to Maine!

● ● ● ● ● ● ● ● ● ● ● ● ● ●

13
brain, cane, chain, crane, drain, gain, grain, lane, main, Maine, mane, pain, pane, plain, plane, rain, reign, rein, sane, Spain, sprain, stain, strain, train, vain, vane, vein

14
faint, paint, quaint, saint

15
ache, bake, brake, break, cake, drake, fake, flake, lake, make, rake, shake, snake, stake, steak, take, wake

● ● ● ● ● ● ● ● ● ● ● ● ● ●

Never bake a snake in a cake,
Unless the snake you bake is fake.

● ● ● ● ● ● ● ● ● ● ● ● ● ●

I knew a boy
who came from France.
He wore silk shirts
and purple pants.
And if you gave him
just a glance,
He'd jump right up
and start to dance.

18
am, clam, cram, dam, gram, ham, jam, lamb, ma'am, ram, scram, slam, swam, tram, wham, yam

19
aim, blame, came, claim, dame, fame, flame, frame, game, lame, name, same, shame, tame

20
camp, champ, clamp, cramp, damp, lamp, ramp, stamp, tramp

21
bran, can, clan, fan, man, pan, plan, ran, scan, tan, than, van

22
chance, chants, dance, France, glance, grants, lance, pants, plants, prance, rants, slants, stance, trance

23
and, band, bland, brand, canned, fanned, gland, grand, hand, land, planned, sand, stand, tanned

16
bald, bawled, brawled, called, crawled, drawled, hauled, scald, scrawled, sprawled, stalled

17
fault, halt, malt, salt, vault

24
bang, clang, fang, gang, hang, rang, sang, slang

25
bank, blank, clank, crank,
drank, frank, plank, prank,
rank, sank, shrank, spank,
stank, swank, tank, thank,
yank

26
ant, aunt, can't, chant, grant,
pant, plant, rant, scant, slant

27
cap, chap, clap, flap, gap, lap,
map, nap, rap, sap, scrap,
slap, snap, strap, tap, trap,
wrap, yap, zap

28
ape, cape, drape, grape,
scrape, shape, tape

29
are, bar, car, far, jar, scar, star,
tar

30
barred, card, guard, hard,
scarred, starred, yard

31
air, bare, bear, blare, care,
chair, dare, fair, fare, flair,
flare, glare, hair, hare, heir,
lair, mare, pair, pare, pear,
rare, scare, share, snare,
spare, square, stair, stare,
swear, tear, their, there,
they're, ware, wear, where

32
barge, charge, large, sarge

● ●

Two bears
Stood on the stairs.
I glared.
They weren't scared.

● ●

"Who's under that mask?"
I started to ask.
Finding it out
Was quite a big task.

33
ark, bark, dark, hark, lark,
mark, park, shark, spark, stark

34
arm, charm, farm, harm

35
art, cart, chart, dart, hart,
heart, part, smart, start, tart

36
ash, bash, cash, clash, crash,
dash, flash, gash, gnash, lash,
rash, smash, splash, trash

37
ask, mask, task

38
bass, brass, class, gas, glass,
grass, lass, mass, pass

39
blast, cast, fast, last, mast,
passed, past, vast

40
chased, faced, haste, laced,
paced, paste, placed, raced,
taste, traced, waist, waste

41
at, bat, brat, cat, chat, fat,
flat, gnat, hat, mat, pat, rat,
sat, spat, that, vat

42
batch, catch, hatch, latch,
match, patch, scratch, snatch

43
ate, crate, date, eight, fate,
freight, gate, great, hate, late,
mate, plate, rate, skate, slate,
state, straight, strait, wait, weight

44
bath, math, path

45
brave, cave, crave, gave,
grave, pave, rave, save, shave,
slave, they've, wave

46
awe, claw, draw, gnaw, jaw,
law, paw, raw, saw, squaw,
straw, thaw

47
all, ball, bawl, brawl, call,
crawl, drawl, fall, hall, haul,
mall, scrawl, shawl, small,
sprawl, squall, stall, tall,
wall

48
dawn, drawn, fawn, gone,
lawn, on, swan, yawn

49
ax, backs, cracks, jacks,
lacks, lax, packs, quacks,
racks, sacks, shacks,
smacks, snacks, stacks,
tacks, tax, tracks, wax,
whacks

50
bay, clay, day, gray, hay,
may, May, pay, play, pray,
prey, ray, say, slay, sleigh,
spray, stay, stray, sway, they,
tray, way, weigh

• •

Wait, wait, till I open the gate,
Then you can skate. You can skate straight.
Don't skate till I open the gate;
Otherwise you won't be skating so great!

• •

51

blaze, days, daze, gaze, glaze,
graze, haze, maize, maze,
pays, phase, phrase, plays,
praise, prays, preys, raise, rays,
slays, sleighs, sprays, stays,
strays, sways, weighs

52

beach, beech, bleach, each,
peach, preach, reach, screech,
speech, teach

53

beak, cheek, creak, creek,
freak, Greek, leak, leek, meek,
peak, peek, seek, sheik, shriek,
sleek, sneak, speak, squeak,
streak, tweak, weak, week

54

deal, eel, feel, heal, heel, he'll,
keel, kneel, meal, peal, peel, real,
reel, seal, she'll, squeal, steal,
steel, veal, we'll, wheel, zeal

Lazy days:
Sun's rays,
Blinding blaze,
Tree sways,
Cows graze,
Warm haze,
Lazy days.

55
beam, cream, dream, gleam,
scheme, scream, seam, seem,
steam, stream, team, theme

56
bean, clean, dean, green, keen,
lean, mean, queen, scene,
screen, seen, sheen, teen

57
beard, cheered, cleared,
feared, neared, smeared,
sneered, steered, weird

58
cease, crease, fleece, geese,
grease, Greece, lease, niece,
peace, piece

59
breeze, cheese, ease, fleas,
flees, frees, freeze, he's, keys,
knees, peas, please, seas, sees,
seize, she's, skis, sneeze,
squeeze, tease, these, trees,
wheeze

60
beast, creased, east, feast,
greased, leased, least, priest,
yeast

61
beat, beet, bleat, cheat, eat,
feat, feet, fleet, greet, heat,
meat, meet, neat, seat, sheet,
sleet, street, suite, sweet,
treat, wheat

● ●

Try not to sneeze when she's up on her skis.
The moment she feels the breeze from your sneeze,
She's liable to bump both her knees on the trees!
So please give your nose just a nice, tweaky squeeze,
And sneeze in the house where your nose cannot freeze!
Thank you.

● ●

62
eve, grieve, leave, sleeve, weave, we've

63
check, deck, fleck, heck, neck, peck, speck, trek, wreck

64
bed, bled, bread, dead, dread, fed, fled, head, lead, led, pled, read, red, said, shed, shred, sled, sped, spread, thread, wed

65
be, bee, fee, flea, flee, free, gee, glee, he, key, knee, me, pea, plea, sea, see, she, ski, spree, tea, three, tree, we, wee

66
bead, bleed, deed, feed, freed, greed, he'd, knead, lead, need, plead, read, reed, seed, she'd, skied, speed, tweed, we'd, weed

67
cheap, cheep, creep, deep, heap, jeep, keep, leap, peep, sheep, sleep, steep, sweep, weep

68
cheer, clear, dear, deer, ear, fear, gear, hear, here, jeer, near, pier, queer, rear, sneer, spear, sphere, steer, tear, year

● ●

If you stay at home in bed,
You will never bump your head
On a pole or sign or tree.
It's safe to stay in bed, you see.

● ●

69
cleft, left, theft

70
beg, egg, keg, leg, peg

71
bell, cell, dell, dwell, fell, sell, shell, smell, spell, swell, tell, well, yell

72
elf, self, shelf

● ● ● ● ● ● ● ● ● ● ● ● ● ● ● ●

On a shelf
by himself
sat an elf.

73
belt, dealt, dwelt, felt, knelt, melt

74
gem, hem, stem, them

75
den, glen, hen, men, pen, ten, then, when, wren

76
cents, dents, fence, rents, scents, sense, tense, tents, vents

77
bend, blend, end, friend, lend, mend, send, spend, tend

78
bent, cent, dent, gent, lent, meant, rent, scent, sent, spent, tent, vent, went

79
pep, prep, step

80
blur, burr, fir, fur, her, purr, sir, slur, spur, stir, were, whir

81
blurb, curb, herb, verb

82
curse, hearse, nurse, purse, verse, worse

● ● ● ● ● ● ● ● ● ● ● ● ● ● ● ●

83
blurt, dirt, flirt, hurt, shirt, skirt, spurt, squirt

84
curve, nerve, serve, swerve, verve

85
bless, chess, dress, guess, less, mess, press, stress, yes

86
best, blessed, blest, chest, crest, dressed, guessed, guest, jest, messed, nest, pest, pressed, quest, rest, test, vest, west, zest

87
bet, debt, fret, get, jet, let, met, net, pet, set, sweat, threat, vet, wet, yet

● ●

Katie Baytee had a curse:
She only spoke in rhymes and verse.
Her mother took her to a nurse,
But after that, her verse got worse.

● ●

Boo hoo.
The bluebird flew.
Up the flue it flew, it's true.
Then it flew right out of view.
That's what bluebirds do to you,
They make you blue.
But then—who knew?

88
etch, fetch, sketch, stretch, wretch

89
blew, blue, boo, brew, chew, clue, coo, crew, cue, dew, do, drew, due, few, flew, flu, flue, glue, goo, grew, knew, moo, new, shoe, stew, threw, through, to, too, true, two, view, who, woo, you, zoo

90
bib, crib, fib, rib

91
dice, ice, lice, mice, nice, price, rice, slice, spice, splice, twice

92
brick, chick, click, flick, kick, lick, nick, pick, quick, sick, stick, thick, tick, trick

In the jungle, Clyde the guide
Spied a tiger near the bride.
"Run and hide!" cried our guy Clyde,
But the tiger ate the bride.
"Well, I tried," sighed Clyde the guide.

93
did, hid, kid, lid, rid, skid,
slid, squid

94
bride, cried, died, dried,
dyed, fried, glide, guide,
hide, lied, pride, pried, ride,
side, sighed, slide, spied, tide,
tied, tried, wide

95
beef, brief, chief, leaf, reef, thief

96
cliff, if, sniff, stiff, whiff

97
knife, life, wife

98
drift, gift, lift, shift, sniffed,
swift, thrift, whiffed

99
big, dig, fig, jig, pig, rig,
sprig, twig

100
bike, dike, hike, like, pike, spike

101
child, filed, mild, piled, smiled, wild

● ● ● ● ● ● ● ● ● ● ● ● ●

Once in a while
I'll walk a mile
To see you smile.

● ● ● ● ● ● ● ● ● ● ● ● ●

102
aisle, file, I'll, isle, mile, pile, smile, tile, vile, while

103
milk, silk

104
bill, chill, dill, fill, gill, grill, hill, ill, kill, mill, pill, quill, sill, skill, spill, still, thrill, til, till, will

105
built, gilt, guilt, hilt, jiit, kilt, quilt, spilt, stilt, tilt, wilt

106
brim, dim, grim, gym, him, hymn, limb, rim, skim, slim, swim, trim, vim, whim

107
chime, climb, crime, dime, grime, I'm, lime, mime, rhyme, slime, time

● ●

Once I had a tiny chimp
Who had a gruesome grin.
And if you called my chimp a "shrimp,"
He'd kick you in the shin.

● ●

108
blimp, chimp, imp, limp,
scrimp, shrimp, skimp

109
been, bin, chin, fin, grin, in,
inn, kin, pin, shin, sin, skin,
spin, thin, tin, twin, win

110
hints, mints, prince, prints,
rinse, since, splints, sprints,
squints, tints, wince

111
cinch, clinch, finch, flinch,
inch, pinch

112
bind, blind, dined, find,
fined, grind, kind, lined,
mind, mined, pined, shined,
signed, whined, wind

113
dine, fine, line, mine, nine,
pine, shine, shrine, sign, spine,
swine, twine, vine, whine,
wine

114
bring, cling, ding, fling, king,
ring, sing, sling, spring, sting,
string, swing, thing, ting,
wing, wring

● ●

My uncle once gave me a strange-looking ring,
Tied up with paper and striped, straggly string.
Pushing the spring made the ring start to sing.
I wonder what next time my uncle will bring.

● ●

115
blink, brink, chink, clink,
drink, ink, kink, link, mink,
pink, rink, shrink, sink, slink,
stink, think, wink, zinc

116
glint, hint, lint, mint, print,
splint, sprint, squint, tint

117
chip, clip, dip, drip, flip, grip,
hip, lip, rip, ship, sip, skip,
slip, snip, strip, tip, trip,
whip, zip

118
gripe, pipe, ripe, stripe, swipe,
type, wipe

119
brier, buyer, choir, fire, flyer,
friar, hire, liar, lyre, mire,
plier, sire, tire, wire

120
firm, germ, squirm, term,
worm

121
berth, birth, earth, mirth,
worth

122
dish, fish, squish, swish, wish

123
brisk, disk, frisk, risk, whisk

● ● ● ● ● ● ● ● ● ● ● ● ● ● ●

Does a worm
Make you squirm?

● ● ● ● ● ● ● ● ● ● ● ● ● ● ●

124
bliss, hiss, kiss, miss, Swiss, this

125
cyst, fist, hissed, kissed, list,
missed, mist, twist, wrist

29

Mama hen had twenty chicks;
Fourteen slept, but six did tricks,
Juggling bricks and dancing kicks,
And making monkeys out of sticks.

126
bit, fit, flit, grit, hit, it, kit,
knit, lit, mitt, nit, pit, quit,
sit, skit, slit, spit, split, wit

127
ditch, hitch, itch, pitch, rich,
snitch, stitch, switch, twitch,
which, witch

128
bite, bright, fight, flight,
fright, height, kite, knight,
light, might, mite, night,
quite, right, sight, slight,
spite, tight, white, write

129
myth, smith, with

130
give, live

131
dive, drive, five, hive, I've,
live, strive

132
bricks, chicks, clicks, fix,
flicks, kicks, licks, mix, nicks,
picks, six, sticks, ticks, tricks

133
fizz, his, is, quiz, 'tis, whiz,
wiz

134
buys, cries, dies, dries, dyes,
eyes, flies, fries, guys, lies,
pries, prize, rise, sighs, size,
wise

135
boast, coast, ghost, host,
most, post, roast, toast

136
blob, bob, cob, glob, job,
knob, lob, mob, nob, rob,
slob, snob, sob, throb

137
globe, lobe, probe, robe

138
block, chalk, chock, clock, cock,
crock, doc, dock, flock, knock,
lock, mock, rock, shock, smock,
sock, stock, tock (ticktock)

139
clod, cod, God, nod, odd,
plod, pod, prod, rod, wad

140
code, flowed, glowed, load,
owed, road, rode, rowed,
sewed, showed, snowed,
stowed, toad, towed

141
dodge, lodge, podge
(hodgepodge)

142
bog, clog, dog, fog, frog,
hog, jog, log

143
boil, broil, coil, foil, oil, soil,
spoil, toil

144
coin, join

145
joint, point

146
boys, joys, noise, toys

147
broke, choke, cloak, Coke,
croak, folk, joke, oak, poke,
soak, spoke, stroke, woke,
yoke, yolk

● ● ● ● ● ● ● ● ● ● ● ● ●

The yolk broke,
And that's no joke!

● ● ● ● ● ● ● ● ● ● ● ● ●

148
bold, bowled, cold, fold,
gold, hold, mold, old, scold,
sold, told

149
bowl, coal, goal, hole, mole,
pole, poll, role, roll, scroll,
sole, soul, stole, stroll, toll,
troll, whole

150
bolt, colt, jolt, volt

151
bomb, prom

152
chrome, comb, dome, foam,
gnome, home, roam, Rome

153
blond, bond, fond, pond, wand

154
blown, bone, cone, flown,
groan, grown, known, loan,
lone, moan, own, phone, sewn,
shone, shown, sown, stone,
throne, thrown, tone, zone

155
gong, long, prong, song,
strong, thong, throng, tong,
wrong

156
could, good, hood, should,
stood, wood, would

157
goof, hoof, proof, roof,
spoof

158
book, brook, cook, crook,
hook, look, shook, took

My dear Joan,
how you have grown!
Your legs are now so long.
My dear Joan,
how time has flown.
It's you—or am I wrong?

159
cool, cruel, drool, fool, fuel,
mule, pool, rule, school,
spool, stool, tool, who'll,
you'll, yule

160
bloom, boom, broom, doom,
gloom, groom, loom, plume,
room, tomb, whom, womb

● ● ● ● ● ● ● ● ● ● ● ● ●

Oh, gloom. Oh, doom.
My mother's giving me the
*   broom,*
And telling me to sweep my
*   room.*

161
croon, dune, goon, June,
loon, moon, noon, prune,
soon, spoon, tune

162
coop, droop, goop, group,
hoop, loop, scoop, soup,
stoop, swoop, troop

163
goose, juice, loose, moose,
noose, spruce, truce, use, Zeus

164
boot, brute, chute, cute, flute,
fruit, hoot, loot, mute, newt,
root, route, shoot, suit, toot

165
foot, put, soot

166
groove, move, prove, who've,
you've

167
blues, boos, brews, bruise,
chews, choose, clues, coos,
crews, cruise, cues, dues, glues,
lose, moos, news, ooze, shoes,
snooze, stews, use, views,
who's, whose, woos, zoos

168
bop, chop, cop, crop, drop,
flop, hop, mop, plop, pop,
prop, shop, slop, stop, swap, top

● ● ● ● ● ● ● ● ● ● ● ● ●

Winter snows,
Gusty blows,
River froze,
Heavy clothes,
Woolen hose,
Snowball throws,
Runny nose,
Frozen toes,
Lamplight glows,
Winter snows.

169
cope, dope, grope, hope,
mope, nope, pope, rope,
slope, soap

170
board, bored, chord, cord,
lord, poured, roared, scored,
snored, soared, stored,
sword, toward

171
boar, bore, chore, core, corps,
door, floor, for, four, lore,
more, oar, or, ore, pore, pour,
roar, score, shore, snore, soar,
sore, store, swore, tore, war,
wore, yore

172
dorm, form, storm, swarm,
warm

173
born, corn, horn, morn,
mourn, scorn, sworn, thorn,
torn, warn, worn

174
coarse, course, force, hoarse,
horse, source

175
court, fort, port, quart,
short, snort, sort, sport, wart

176
close, dose, gross

177
blows, chose, close, clothes,
crows, does, doze, flows,
foes, froze, glows, goes,
hose, knows, mows, nose,
owes, pose, prose, rose,
rows, sews, shows, slows,
snows, sows, stows, those,
throws, toes, tows

178
boss, cross, gloss, loss, moss,
sauce, toss

179
cost, frost, lost

180
blot, clot, cot, dot, got, hot,
jot, knot, lot, not, plot, pot,
rot, shot, slot, spot, squat,
tot, trot, watt, yacht

181
blotch, botch, notch, splotch,
swatch, watch

182
boat, coat, float, goat, note,
oat, quote, throat, vote, wrote

183
broth, cloth, froth, moth

184
both, growth, oath

185
couch, crouch, grouch, ouch,
pouch, slouch

186
bowed, cloud, crowd, loud,
plowed, proud, vowed,
wowed

Once there was a seafaring goat
Who spent all his days and his nights on a boat.
Then the boat hit a tree
And he fell in the sea
And learned very fast
	that goats do not float.

187
bought, brought, caught,
fought, ought, sought,
taught, taut, thought

188
bounce, counts, mounts,
ounce, pounce, trounce

189
bound, clowned, crowned,
drowned, found, frowned,
ground, hound, mound,
pound, round, sound,
wound

190
crooned, pruned, swooned,
tuned, wound

191
flour, flower, hour, our,
power, shower, sour, tower

192
blouse, house, louse, mouse,
spouse

193
bout, doubt, drought, out,
pout, scout, shout, snout,
spout, sprout, stout, trout

194
dove, glove, love, of, shove

195
dove, drove, grove, stove, wove

● ● ● ● ● ● ● ● ● ● ● ●

Spouse Finds Mouse in House!

● ● ● ● ● ● ● ● ● ● ● ●

196
bough, bow, brow, chow,
cow, how, now, plow, pow,
sow, vow, wow

197
blow, bow, crow, doe,
dough, flow, foe, glow, go,
grow, hoe, know, low, mow,
no, oh, owe, row, sew, show,
slow, snow, so, sow, stow,
throw, toe, tow, whoa, woe

198
foul, fowl, growl, howl, owl,
prowl, scowl

199
brown, clown, crown, down,
drown, frown, gown, noun,
town

200
blocks, box, clocks, docks,
flocks, fox, frocks, knocks,
locks, lox, mocks, ox, pox,
rocks, shocks, smocks, socks,
sox, stocks

201
boy, joy, toy

202
club, cub, grub, rub, scrub,
shrub, snub, stub, sub, tub

203
buck, chuck, cluck, duck, luck,
pluck, puck, struck, stuck,
suck, truck, tuck

204
blood, bud, cud, dud, flood,
mud, spud, thud

• •

"Oh, joy! Oh, joy!"
Cried the girl and the boy.
"Mama has bought us our favorite toy.
It isn't socks.
It isn't frocks.
It's a bulging box of building blocks!"

• •

Huff huff,
You're not so tough;
You think you're such a scary stuff.
Huff huff,
You're not so rough;
You're just a big bamboozling bluff.
Huff huff,
You're not so gruff;
You're just a piece of flimsy fluff.

205
booed, brewed, brood,
chewed, cooed, crude, dude,
feud, food, mood, mooed,
rude, stewed, sued, viewed,
who'd, wooed, you'd

206
budge, drudge, fudge,
grudge, judge, nudge,
sludge, smudge, trudge

207
bluff, cuff, fluff, gruff, guff,
huff, muff, puff, rough, scuff,
stuff, tough

208
bug, chug, drug, dug, hug,
jug, lug, mug, plug, rug,
shrug, snug, thug, tug

209
bulk, hulk, skulk, sulk

210
dull, gull, hull, lull, skull

211
bull, full, pull, wool

212
chum, come, crumb, drum,
from, gum, hum, numb,
plum, slum, some, strum,
sum, swum, thumb

213
bump, chump, clump,
dump, grump, hump,
jump, lump, plump, pump,
slump, stump, thump,
ump

214
bun, done, fun, gun, none,
nun, one, pun, run, shun,
son, spun, stun, sun, ton,
won

215
bunts, dunce, grunts, hunts,
once, punts, stunts

216
brunch, bunch, crunch, hunch,
lunch, munch, punch, scrunch

217
clung, flung, hung, lung,
rung, slung, sprung, strung,
stung, sung, swung, tongue,
young

• •

Bananas growing by the bunch
In the morning sun;
Pick one, peel one, for your lunch,
And eat it in a bun.

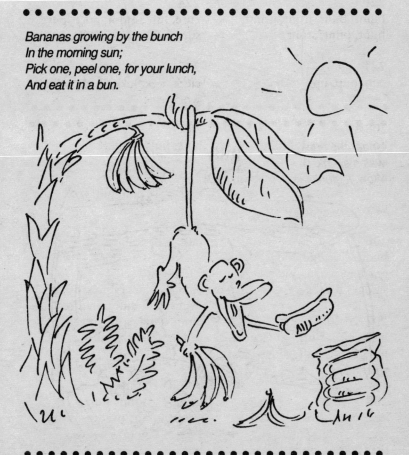

• •

218
lunge, plunge, sponge

219
bunk, chunk, drunk, dunk,
flunk, hunk, junk, monk,
plunk, punk, shrunk, skunk,
spunk, stunk, sunk, trunk

220
blunt, bunt, front, grunt,
hunt, punt, stunt

221
cup, pup, up

222
birch, church, lurch, perch,
search

223
bird, blurred, heard, herd,
purred, slurred, spurred,
stirred, third, whirred, word

224
cure, lure, moor, poor, pure,
sure, tour, your, you're

225
clerk, jerk, lurk, shirk, smirk,
work

* *

*Under the bunk
was a skunk.
Wow, it stunk!*

* *

Said the bird up in the sky,
As he flew away up high,
"I don't know exactly why,
But I have to say good-bye."

226
curl, girl, hurl, pearl, swirl,
twirl, whirl

227
burn, churn, earn, fern, learn,
stern, turn, urn, yearn

228
burp, chirp

229
burst, cursed, first, nursed,
thirst, worst

230
bus, cuss, fuss, muss, plus,
us

231
blush, brush, crush, flush,
gush, hush, mush, rush,
shush, slush, thrush

232
bush, push

233
bussed, bust, crust, cussed,
dust, fussed, gust, just, mussed,
must, rust, thrust, trust

234
but, butt, cut, gut, hut, jut, mutt,
nut, putt, rut, shut, strut, what

235
crutch, much, such, touch

236
buzz, does, fuzz

237
buy, by, bye, cry, die, dry,
dye, eye, fly, fry, guy, hi, high,
I, lie, lye, my, pie, pry, rye,
shy, sigh, sky, sly, spry, spy,
sty, thigh, tie, try, why, wry

Alphabetical List

of the Rhyming Words in This Book

Alphabetical List
of the Rhyming Words in This Book

WORD	PAGE	GROUP	WORD	PAGE	GROUP
band	16	23	bear	17	31
bang	16	24	beard	21	57
bank	17	25	beast	21	60
bar	17	29	beat	21	61
bare	17	31	bed	22	64
barge	17	32	bee	22	65
bark	18	33	beech	20	52
barred	17	30	beef	26	95
base	14	3	been	28	109
bash	18	36	beet	21	61
bass (rhymes with face)	14	3	beg	23	70
bass (rhymes with class)	18	38	bell	23	71
bat	18	41	belt	23	73
batch	18	42	bend	23	77
bath	18	44	bent	23	78
bawl	19	47	berth	29	121
bawled	16	16	best	24	86
bay	19	50	bet	24	87
be	22	65	bib	25	90
beach	20	52	big	26	99
bead	22	66	bike	27	100
beak	20	53	bill	27	104
beam	21	55	bin	28	109
bean	21	56	bind	28	112

WORD	PAGE	GROUP	WORD	PAGE	GROUP
birch	40	222	blind	28	112
bird	40	223	blink	29	115
birth	29	121	bliss	29	124
bit	30	126	blob	31	136
bite	30	128	block	31	138
blab	14	2	blocks	37	200
black	14	4	blond	32	153
blade	14	7	blood	37	204
blah	14	1	bloom	33	160
blame	16	19	blot	35	180
bland	16	23	blotch	35	181
blank	17	25	blouse	36	192
blare	17	31	blow	36	197
blast	18	39	blown	32	154
blaze	20	51	blows	35	177
bleach	20	52	blue	25	89
bleat	21	61	blues	33	167
bled	22	64	bluff	38	207
bleed	22	66	blunt	40	220
blend	23	77	blur	23	80
bless	24	85	blurb	23	81
blessed	24	86	blurred	40	223
blest	24	86	blurt	24	83
blew	25	89	blush	41	231
blimp	28	108	boar	34	171

WORD	PAGE	GROUP	WORD	PAGE	GROUP
board	34	170	bought	36	187
boast	30	135	bounce	36	188
boat	35	182	bound	36	189
bob	31	136	bout	36	193
bog	31	142	bow (rhymes with cow)	36	196
boil	31	143	bow (rhymes with go)	36	197
bold	31	148	bowed	35	186
bolt	32	150	bowl	31	149
bomb	32	151	bowled	31	148
bond	32	153	box	37	200
bone	32	154	boy	37	201
boo	25	89	boys	31	146
booed	38	205	brace	14	3
book	32	158	brag	15	10
boom	33	160	braid	14	7
boos	33	167	braille	15	12
boot	33	164	brain	15	13
bop	33	168	brake	15	15
bore	34	171	bran	16	21
bored	34	170	brand	16	23
born	34	173	brass	18	38
boss	35	178	brat	18	41
botch	35	181	brave	18	45
both	35	184	brawl	19	47
bough	36	196	brawled	16	16

WORD	PAGE	GROUP	WORD	PAGE	GROUP
clank	17	25	close	35	177
			rhymes with rose		
clap	17	27	clot	35	180
clash	18	36	cloth	35	183
class	18	38	clothes	35	177
claw	19	46	cloud	35	186
clay	19	50	clown	37	199
clean	21	56	clowned	36	189
clear	22	68	club	37	202
cleared	21	57	cluck	37	203
cleft	23	69	clue	25	89
clerk	40	225	clues	33	167
click	25	92	clump	38	213
clicks	30	132	clung	39	217
cliff	26	96	coal	31	149
climb	27	107	coarse	34	174
clinch	28	111	coast	30	135
cling	28	114	coat	35	182
clink	29	115	cob	31	136
clip	29	117	cock	31	138
cloak	31	147	cod	31	139
clock	31	138	code	31	140
clocks	37	200	coil	31	143
clod	31	139	coin	31	144
clog	31	142	Coke	31	147
close	34	176	cold	31	148
rhymes with gross					

D

WORD	PAGE	GROUP	WORD	PAGE	GROUP
force	34	174	frisk	29	123
form	34	172	frocks	37	200
fort	34	175	frog	31	142
fought	36	187	from	38	212
foul	37	198	front	40	220
found	36	189	frost	35	179
four	34	171	froth	35	183
fowl	37	198	frown	37	199
fox	37	200	frowned	36	189
frail	15	12	froze	35	177
frame	16	19	fruit	33	164
France	16	22	fry	41	237
frank	17	25	fudge	38	206
freak	20	53	fuel	33	159
free	22	65	full	38	211
freed	22	66	fun	39	214
frees	21	59	fur	23	80
freeze	21	59	fuss	41	230
freight	18	43	fussed	41	233
fret	24	87	fuzz	41	236
friar	29	119			
fried	26	94	gab	14	2
friend	23	77	gag	15	10
fries	30	134	gain	15	13
fright	30	128	gale	15	12

G

WORD	PAGE	GROUP	WORD	PAGE	GROUP
game	16	19	gland	16	23
gang	16	24	glare	17	31
gap	17	27	glass	18	38
gas	18	38	glaze	20	51
gash	18	36	gleam	21	55
gate	18	43	glee	22	65
gauge	15	11	glen	23	75
gave	18	45	glide	26	94
gaze	20	51	glint	29	116
gear	22	68	glob	31	136
gee	22	65	globe	31	137
geese	21	58	gloom	33	160
gem	23	74	gloss	35	178
gent	23	78	glove	36	194
germ	29	120	glow	36	197
get	24	87	glowed	31	140
ghost	30	135	glows	35	177
gift	26	98	glue	25	89
gill	27	104	glues	33	167
gilt	27	105	gnash	18	36
girl	41	226	gnat	18	41
give	30	130	gnaw	19	46
glad	14	6	gnome	32	152
glade	14	7	go	36	197
glance	16	22	goal	31	149

H

J

K

M

N

O

Q

R

WORD	PAGE	GROUP	WORD	PAGE	GROUP
sleighs	20	51	sly	41	237
slice	25	91	smack	14	4
slid	26	93	smacked	14	5
slide	26	94	smacks	19	49
slight	30	128	small	19	47
slim	27	106	smart	18	35
slime	27	107	smash	18	36
sling	28	114	smeared	21	57
slink	29	115	smell	23	71
slip	29	117	smile	27	102
slit	30	126	smiled	27	101
slob	31	136	smirk	40	225
slop	33	168	smith	30	129
slope	34	169	smock	31	138
slot	35	180	smocks	37	200
slouch	35	185	smudge	38	206
slow	36	197	snack	14	4
slows	35	177	snacked	14	5
sludge	38	206	snacks	19	49
slum	38	212	snag	15	10
slump	38	213	snail	15	12
slung	39	217	snake	15	15
slur	23	80	snap	17	27
slurred	40	223	snare	17	31
slush	41	231	snatch	18	42

WORD	PAGE	GROUP	WORD	PAGE	GROUP
stream	21	55	sub	37	202
street	21	61	such	41	235
stress	24	85	suck	37	203
stretch	25	88	sued	38	205
string	28	114	suit	33	164
strip	29	117	suite	21	61
stripe	29	118	sulk	38	209
strive	30	131	sum	38	212
stroke	31	147	sun	39	214
stroll	31	149	sung	39	217
strong	32	155	sunk	40	219
struck	37	203	sure	40	224
strum	38	212	swam	16	18
strung	39	217	swan	19	48
strut	41	234	swank	17	25
stub	37	202	swap	33	168
stuck	37	203	swarm	34	172
stuff	38	207	swatch	35	181
stump	38	213	sway	19	50
stun	39	214	swayed	14	7
stung	39	217	sways	20	51
stunk	40	219	swear	17	31
stunt	40	220	sweat	24	87
stunts	39	215	sweep	22	67
sty	41	237	sweet	21	61

y

WORD   PAGE   GROUP